Hello, Truman!

Todd Donoho

Illustrated by Edson Saenz

www.mascotbooks.com

Hello, I am Truman the Tiger.
I am the proud mascot of the
University of Missouri.

I am named after Harry S. Truman, the only United States President born and raised in the state of Missouri.

It's a football game day in Columbia, Missouri. On my way to the stadium, I like to walk through campus.

I start my journey at the Columns in front of Jesse Hall. I see many students and alumni who say, "Hello, Truman!"

My next stop is Memorial Union,
my favorite building on campus.

Outside Memorial Union, I run into a few more students. Everyone cheers, "Hello, Truman!"

Tiger Plaza is my next stop.
The Plaza is a great place to
take pictures.

Tiger fans love to take pictures with me.
"Hello, Truman!" say Tiger fans.

Before I know it, I arrive at Greektown. This is where the fraternity and sorority houses are. Many students live here.

The houses are decorated on game day, especially for homecoming. Mizzou has one of the oldest homecomings of any college.

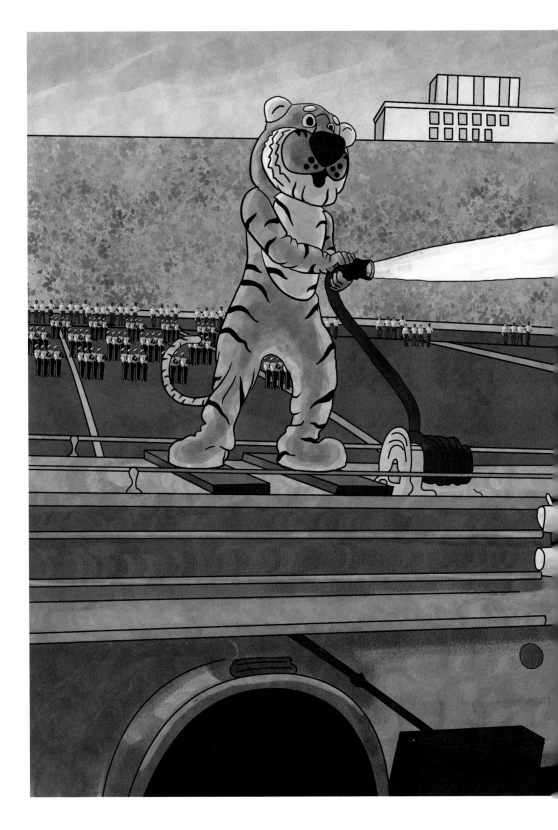

Finally, I arrive at Faurot Field, home of the Tigers. I make my entrance on a big yellow fire truck.

On hot days, I soak the crowd
with water. The fans yell,
"Hello, Truman!"

I help the Marching Mizzou Band
with our school fight songs,
Every True Son and *Fight Tiger*.

During *The Missouri Waltz,* fans sway
their arms to the music.

During the game, I also help our cheerleaders. Our favorite cheer is the M-I-Z Z-O-U cheer.

One side of the stadium yells, "M-I-Z!" The other side of the stadium yells back, "Z-O-U!"

When the Tigers score a touchdown,
a cannon is fired, and I do a push-up
for every point scored by the team.

If the Tigers score 40 points, I
do 40 push-ups. Truman has
to be in good shape!

On this day, Mizzou scored lots of points and won the game. I gave the coach and all the players a high-five after the game.

I love to celebrate Tiger victories with the football team and our fans. The players say, "Great game, Truman!"

After the game, I get hugs from many Tiger fans. I especially love the youngest Tiger fans.

That's the best way to end a game day
at the University of Missouri in Columbia.

To the next generation of Mizzou fans, students and alumni. As the saying goes, you graduate from the University of Missouri, but Tiger spirit never leaves you. Forever Mizzou! ~ Todd Donoho

Dedicated to God for His mercy and kindness, to my family for their love and support. ~ Edson Saenz

For more information about our products, please visit us online at www.mascotbooks.com.

For more information, please contact Mascot Books,
P.O. Box 220157, Chantilly, VA 20153-0157

ISBN: 978-1-932888-57-7

Printed in the United States.

Title List

Team	Book Title	Author	Team	Book Title	Author
Baseball			**Pro Football**		
Boston Red Sox	Hello, Wally!	Jerry Remy	Carolina Panthers	Let's Go, Panthers!	Aimee Aryal
Boston Red Sox	Wally And His Journey Through Red Sox Nation!	Jerry Remy	Dallas Cowboys	How 'Bout Them Cowboys!	Aimee Aryal
New York Yankees	Let's Go, Yankees!	Yogi Berra	Green Bay Packers	Go, Packres, Go!	Aimee Aryal
New York Mets	Hello, Mr. Met!	Rusty Staub	Kansas City Chiefs	Let's Go, Chiefs!	Aimee Aryal
St. Louis Cardinals	Hello, Fredbird!	Ozzie Smith	Minnesota Vikings	Let's Go, Vikings!	Aimee Aryal
Philadelphia Phillies	Hello, Phillie Phanatic!	Aimee Aryal	New York Giants	Let's Go, Giants!	Aimee Aryal
Chicago Cubs	Let's Go, Cubs!	Aimee Aryal	New England Patriots	Let's Go, Patriots!	Aimee Aryal
Chicago White Sox	Let's Go, White Sox!	Aimee Aryal	Seattle Seahawks	Let's Go, Seahawks!	Aimee Aryal
Cleveland Indians	Hello, Slider!	Bob Feller	Washington Redskins	Hail To The Redskins!	Aimee Aryal
			Coloring Book		
			Dallas Cowboys	How 'Bout Them Cowboys!	Aimee Aryal
College					
Alabama	Hello, Big Al!	Aimee Aryal	Michigan State	Hello, Sparty!	Aimee Aryal
Alabama	Roll Tide!	Ken Stabler	Minnesota	Hello, Goldy!	Aimee Aryal
Arizona	Hello, Wilbur!	Lute Olsen	Mississippi	Hello, Colonel Rebel!	Aimee Aryal
Arkansas	Hello, Big Red!	Aimee Aryal	Mississippi State	Hello, Bully!	Aimee Aryal
Auburn	Hello, Aubie!	Aimee Aryal	Missouri	Hello, Truman!	Todd Donoho
Auburn	War Eagle!	Pat Dye	Nebraska	Hello, Herbie Husker!	Aimee Aryal
Boston College	Hello, Baldwin!	Aimee Aryal	North Carolina	Hello, Rameses!	Aimee Aryal
Brigham Young	Hello, Cosmo!	LaVell Edwards	North Carolina St.	Hello, Mr. Wuf!	Aimee Aryal
Clemson	Hello, Tiger!	Aimee Aryal	Notre Dame	Let's Go, Irish!	Aimee Aryal
Colorado	Hello, Ralphie!	Aimee Aryal	Ohio State	Hello, Brutus!	Aimee Aryal
Connecticut	Hello, Jonathan!	Aimee Aryal	Oklahoma	Let's Go, Sooners!	Aimee Aryal
Duke	Hello, Blue Devil!	Aimee Aryal	Oklahoma State	Hello, Pistol Pete!	Aimee Aryal
Florida	Hello, Albert!	Aimee Aryal	Penn State	Hello, Nittany Lion!	Aimee Aryal
Florida State	Let's Go, 'Noles!	Aimee Aryal	Penn State	We Are Penn State!	Joe Paterno
Georgia	Hello, Hairy Dawg!	Aimee Aryal	Purdue	Hello, Purdue Pete!	Aimee Aryal
Georgia	How 'Bout Them Dawgs!	Vince Dooley	Rutgers	Hello, Scarlet Knight!	Aimee Aryal
Georgia Tech	Hello, Buzz!	Aimee Aryal	South Carolina	Hello, Cocky!	Aimee Aryal
Illinois	Let's Go, Illini!	Aimee Aryal	So. California	Hello, Tommy Trojan!	Aimee Aryal
Indiana	Let's Go, Hoosiers!	Aimee Aryal	Syracuse	Hello, Otto!	Aimee Aryal
Iowa	Hello, Herky!	Aimee Aryal	Tennessee	Hello, Smokey!	Aimee Aryal
Iowa State	Hello, Cy!	Amy DeLashmutt	Texas	Hello, Hook 'Em!	Aimee Aryal
James Madison	Hello, Duke Dog!	Aimee Aryal	Texas A & M	Howdy, Reveille!	Aimee Aryal
Kansas	Hello, Big Jay!	Aimee Aryal	UCLA	Hello, Joe Bruin!	Aimee Aryal
Kansas State	Hello, Willie!	Dan Walter	Virginia	Hello, CavMan!	Aimee Aryal
Kentucky	Hello, Wildcat!	Aimee Aryal	Virginia Tech	Hello, Hokie Bird!	Aimee Aryal
Louisiana State	Hello, Mike!	Aimee Aryal	Virginia Tech	Yea, It's Hokie Game Day!	Frank Beamer
Maryland	Hello, Testudo!	Aimee Aryal	Wake Forest	Hello, Demon Deacon!	Aimee Aryal
Michigan	Let's Go, Blue!	Aimee Aryal	West Virginia	Hello, Mountaineer!	Aimee Aryal
			Wisconsin	Hello, Bucky!	Aimee Aryal
NBA					
Dallas Mavericks	Let's Go, Mavs!	Mark Cuban			
Kentucky Derby					
Kentucky Derby	White Diamond Runs For The Roses	Aimee Aryal			

More great titles coming soon!